THE RED HEN

THE RED HEN

BY REBECCA EMBERLEY
AND
ED EMBERLEY

A NEAL PORTER BOOK
ROARING BROOK PRESS
NEW YORK

One beautiful morning the Red Hen found
a wonderful recipe for a cake.

"This would be a treat for all of us," she thought.

SIMPLY
SPLENDID
CAKE

"This cake should be baked. Who will help me gather the ingredients?" she asked.

"Not I," said the cat.

"Not I," said the rat.

"Bribbit," said the frog.

"All right then, I shall do it myself."
And she did.

"Now I have everything we need, who will help me mix the cake?" she asked.

"Not I," said the cat.

"Not I," said the rat.

"Bribbit," said the frog.

"All right then, I shall do it myself."
And she did.

"Now the cake is all mixed, who will help me bake the cake?" she asked.

"Not I," said the cat.

"Not I," said the rat.

"Bribbit," said the frog.

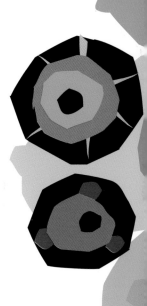

"All right then, I shall do it myself."
And she did.

The cake came out of the oven golden and sweet.
"Who will help me ice the cake?" she asked.

"Not I," said the cat.

"Not I," said the rat.

"Bribbit," said the frog.

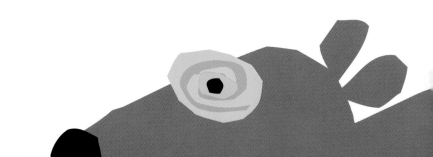

"All right then," she sighed. "I will do it myself."
And she did.

"Now the cake is iced, who will help me decorate the cake?" she asked.
She pretty much knew what was coming …

"Not I," said the cat.

"Not I," said the rat.

"Bribbit," said the frog.

"All right then, I shall do it myself."
And she did.

"This cake looks splendid!" said the Red Hen.
"Who will help me eat the cake?"

"I will!" said the cat.

"I will!" said the rat.

"Bribbit ribbit!" said the frog.

"Hmmph!" said the Red Hen. "I think I will eat it myself."
And she did.

RED HEN'S SIMPLY SPLENDID CAKE

Makes 12 cupcakes or one 9-inch cake

INGREDIENTS

1 cup sugar

½ cup butter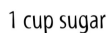

2 eggs

2 teaspoons vanilla extract

1 ½ cups all-purpose flour

1 ¾ teaspoons baking powder

½ cup milk

DIRECTIONS

1. With a grownup's help, preheat oven to 350 degrees. Grease and flour a 9-inch pan or line a muffin pan with paper liners.

2. In a medium bowl, cream together the sugar and butter. Beat in the eggs, one at a time, then stir in the vanilla. Combine flour and baking powder, add to the creamed mixture and mix well. Finally, stir in the milk until batter is smooth. Pour or spoon batter into the prepared pan.

3. Bake for 30 to 40 minutes in the preheated oven. For cupcakes, bake for 20 to 25 minutes. Cake is done when golden and top springs back to the touch.

Copyright © 2009 by Rebecca Emberley Inc.

A Neal Porter Book

Published by Roaring Brook Press

Roaring Brook Press is a division of Holtzbrinck Publishing Holdings Limited Partnership

175 Fifth Avenue, New York, New York 10010

www.roaringbrookpress.com

Distributed in Canada by H.B. Fenn and Company Ltd.

Cataloging-in-Publication Data is on file at the Library of Congress.

ISBN: 978-1-59643-492-9

Roaring Brook Press books are available for special promotions and premiums.

For details contact: Director of Special Markets, Holtzbrinck Publishers.

First Edition November 2010

Printed in July 2010 in China by South China Printing Co. Ltd., Dongguan City, Guangdong Province

1   3   5   7   9   10   8   6   4   2